EARTH DAY

Katie Gillespie

www.av2books.com

LET'S READ AV² BY WEIGL™
ADDED VALUE • AUDIO VISUAL

Go to **www.av2books.com**, and enter this book's unique code.

BOOK CODE

K382689

AV² by Weigl brings you media enhanced books that support active learning.

AV² provides enriched content that supplements and complements this book. Weigl's AV² books strive to create inspired learning and engage young minds in a total learning experience.

Your AV² Media Enhanced books come alive with...

Audio
Listen to sections of the book read aloud.

Video
Watch informative video clips.

Embedded Weblinks
Gain additional information for research.

Try This!
Complete activities and hands-on experiments.

Key Words
Study vocabulary, and complete a matching word activity.

Quizzes
Test your knowledge.

Slide Show
View images and captions, and prepare a presentation.

... and much, much more!

Published by AV² by Weigl
350 5th Avenue, 59th Floor
New York, NY 10118

Website: www.av2books.com

Library of Congress Control Number: 2017930492

ISBN 978-1-4896-5905-7 (hardcover)
ISBN 978-1-4896-5906-4 (softcover)
ISBN 978-1-4896-5907-1 (multi-user eBook)

Printed in the United States of America in Brainerd, Minnesota
1 2 3 4 5 6 7 8 9 0 21 20 19 18 17

022017
020317

Editor: Katie Gillespie   Designer: Ana María Vidal

Weigl acknowledges Getty Images and iStock as the primary image suppliers for this title.

CONTENTS

3

Earth Day is celebrated on April 22 every year.

It is a day to get people involved in cleaning up the planet.

Earth Day has been celebrated for almost 50 years.

It was started to find ways to protect Earth for the future.

Earth Day Network brings people together to help the planet. One of its most important goals is to plant trees around the world.

Earth Day Network wants to plant **7.8 billion** trees by the **year 2020**.

The first Earth Day celebrations took place across America on April 22, 1970. The biggest events were held in Washington, D.C., and New York City.

About **20 million** Americans took part in events on the **first** Earth Day.

People come together on Earth Day. They work toward cleaner land, water, and air.

One way to celebrate Earth Day is to spread awareness. It is important to teach others how to take care of Earth.

Earth Day is celebrated in **192** different countries today.

Some people hold recycling drives on Earth Day.

Plastic, paper, and cardboard can all be recycled.

Many people volunteer on Earth Day. They pull weeds in parks or pick up litter at local schools.

Even small changes can make a big difference. People can help by turning off the lights when they leave a room.

More than **1 billion** people now celebrate **Earth Day** each year.

EARTH DAY FACTS

This page provides more details about the interesting facts found in the book. They are intended to be used by adults as a learning support to help young readers round out their knowledge of each celebration featured in the *Coming Together to Celebrate* series.

Pages 4–5

Earth Day is celebrated on April 22 every year. The idea first came from U.S. Senator Gaylord Nelson. He was inspired to take action after an oil spill in Santa Barbara, California. Nelson was awarded the Presidential Medal of Freedom in 1995 for founding Earth Day. That is the highest honor an American civilian can be given.

Pages 6–7

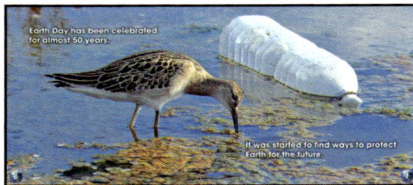

Earth Day has been celebrated for almost 50 years. In 1970, Nelson recruited Denis Hayes as Earth Day's national coordinator. Along with a staff of 85 people across the United States, Hayes promoted Earth Day events to raise awareness about air and water pollution. In 1990, Hayes organized another campaign, which helped Earth Day become a global event. Today, Earth Day events encourage environmental protection all over the planet.

Pages 8–9

Earth Day Network brings people together to help the planet. This group formed to help the environment after the first Earth Day. Earth Day Network wants to plant 7.8 billion trees by Earth Day's 50th anniversary in 2020. That is one tree for every person on the planet. Planting trees was chosen as a goal because trees help communities, combat climate change, and provide clean air to breathe.

Pages 10–11

The first Earth Day celebrations took place across America on April 22, 1970. People gathered at schools, parks, and auditoriums all over the country in support of a healthy and sustainable environment. Earth Day 1970 led to crucial developments, such as the creation of the United States Environmental Protection Agency, as well as the passage of the Clean Air, Clean Water, and Endangered Species Acts.

People come together on Earth Day. Community gardening produces healthy food, lowers family meal costs, and encourages social interaction. People also come together to support local farmer's markets. Buying locally cuts down the distance food must travel, which conserves resources and reduces pollution.

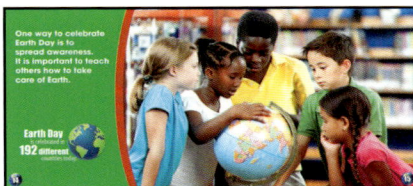

One way to celebrate Earth Day is to spread awareness. People can make phone calls or post on social media about how to make a difference. One way is to stop using unnecessary plastic. Only about 10 percent of the plastic bags, bottles, and other packages made each year are properly recycled. Switching to refillable drinking containers and reusable grocery bags reduces the need for disposable plastic.

Some people hold recycling drives on Earth Day. Aluminium cans are 100 percent recyclable, but only about half of the cans that are used actually get recycled. People can get involved by collecting cans and other materials for recycling. Many common household items can be recycled, including magazines, newspapers, juice cartons, soda bottles, light bulbs, and batteries.

Many people volunteer on Earth Day. One of the most popular ways to help out is to clean up parks or maintain community trails. Volunteering on Earth Day may make people realize that the environment needs to be protected all year, not just on April 22nd. This can lead to other important actions, such as planting flowers in the neighborhood or picking up garbage at local schools.

Even small changes can make a big difference. There are countless ways to save energy. People can contribute by making small changes to their everyday routines. For example, not leaving the faucet running while brushing your teeth helps to save water. By carpooling or using public transportation, such as buses and trains, people can also help to conserve energy.

KEY WORDS

Research has shown that as much as 65 percent of all written material published in English is made up of 300 words. These 300 words cannot be taught using pictures or learned by sounding them out. They must be recognized by sight. This book contains 75 common sight words to help young readers improve their reading fluency and comprehension. This book also teaches young readers several important content words. These words are paired with pictures to aid in learning and improve understanding.

Page	Sight Words First Appearance
4	day, earth, every, is, on, year
5	a, get, in, it, people, the, to, up
6	almost, been, for, has
7	find, started, was, ways
8	around, by, help, important, its, most, of, one, plant, together, trees, wants, world
11	about, America, and, first, part, place, took, were
12	air, come, land, they, water, work
14	different, how, others, take
16	some
17	all, be, can, paper
19	at, many, or, schools
21	big, changes, each, even, leave, lights, make, more, now, off, small, than, when

Page	Content Words First Appearance
4	April
5	planet
7	future
8	Earth Day Network, goals
11	celebrations, events, New York City, Washington, D.C.
14	awareness, countries
16	recycling drives
17	cardboard, plastic
19	parks, litter, weeds
21	difference, room

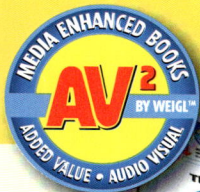

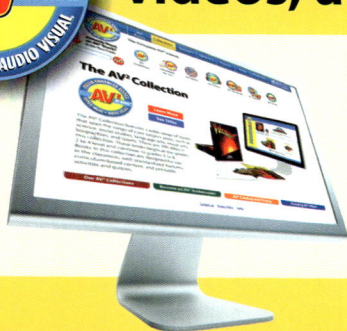

24